REDMOND'S SHOT

REDMOND'S SHOT

Dan J. Marlowe

Fearon
BELMONT, CALIFORNIA

FASTBACK® SPORTS BOOKS

Claire

The Comeback

Game Day

The Kid with the Left Hook

Marathon

Markers

Redmond's Shot

The Rookie

The Sure Thing

Turk

Cover photographer: Kevy Kennedy

ISBN—0-8224-6498-5

Printed in the United States of America.

1. 9 8 7 6 5 4 3

Flint Redmond skated in a tight little circle in front of the starting team's goal. His rangy, six-foot, 190-pound, eighteen-year-old body looked bulky in the hockey uniform. Larry Russo, Flint's best friend and the Junior Mantas' graceful center, swooped past in a rush. "Come early to the party," he said.

"Okay," Flint called after him. Larry was already halfway across the rink.

Coach Bob Carpenter's whistle sounded

loudly. "All right!" he barked. His hoarse voice echoed in the small, empty arena. "Let's knock off a few power plays! Second line on offense, first line on defense. Larry, you sit out the first shift."

Larry went to the penalty box, passing the silent extra players standing against the side boards. Flint went to his position at left defense. In a straight line across from him was his defensive partner, Emile Cartier. Flint glanced over his shoulder at goalie Tom Pollock. Skinny Tom whacked his big stick down upon the ice to show he was ready.

The coach's whistle blasted again. He slid the puck in his hand just inside the defensive blue line to Hank Wilson, the second line's right winger. Wilson promptly drove it across the ice to Roy Eberhardt, the left winger. Frenchy Lalonde and Bryan Park, Flint's wings, edged backward slowly until, with Flint and Emile, they formed a box.

Jean Fitzroy, the second line's center, skated inside the box. He turned to look for a pass. Instead, Eberhardt took two long, slashing strides toward the goal and shot the puck. Fitzroy at once headed toward the goal, but Flint shouldered him aside. He steered Fitzroy wide of the net, away from a possible rebound.

But there was no rebound. Pollock saved the shot cleanly and cleared it to Emile. The chunky French Canadian fired it up the ice where it hit the right boards and circled behind the attackers' goal.

Carl Dupont, the Mantas' other goalie, dug it out and then the whistle blew again.

"All right, all right!" Carpenter shouted. "Sharpen up. Down here again!"

They practiced it a dozen more times. They took turns sitting out as the supposed penalized player. Only once did the offensive line succeed in scoring. Pollock flopped to the ice, and Eberhardt snared the rebound and fired it over him into the goal.

"Time!" Carpenter said finally. "Same time tomorrow. We'll practice a few offensive face-offs in the opponent's end."

The team skated through the gate in the boards, and clumped along the wooden walkway to the dressing room. Equipment flew in all directions as the players tried to be first under the four lukewarm showers.

The arena was empty in fifteen minutes.

Flint arrived at Mrs. Ward's house, where Larry lived, at seven o'clock that evening. Larry's eighteenth birthday party, given by Mrs. Ward and the other women who housed Mantas' players, was scheduled for seven-thirty. Mrs. Fox, Flint's landlady, had had an eighteenth birthday party for Flint three weeks earlier.

Flint turned on the front porch at the

sound of footsteps behind him. Louis Goulet, the sportswriter for the *Reardon Times* was right behind him. Reardon was the town that supported the Junior Mantas, who were just one step below the National Hockey League.

"Ah, there!" Goulet greeted Flint. "We're both early. I wanted to have a word with Larry." They both went inside into a medium-sized dining room, where Mrs. Ward was arranging the food on a large table.

Larry carefully carried a full punch bowl to the table and set it down. Goulet drew Larry aside and spoke to him. Flint could see Larry nodding his head several times in agreement.

"What was that about?"Flint asked

Larry, when the conversation broke up and Goulet went over to speak to Mrs. Ward.

Larry looked embarrassed. "Goulet said there'll be an NHL scout at the game Wednesday night."

Larry Ruso was the Mantas' star player and the local fans' favorite. "That's great, Larry!" Flint said warmly. "I'm sure you'll be drafted."

"I really don't want to play another year in the juniors," Larry admitted. "I think I'm ready, but whether *they'll* think I'm ready . . . ," his voice trailed off. "Anyway, he'll be looking at you, too. And maybe Emile."

"But it's you he's coming to see," Flint pointed out.

"Sometimes I wish we hadn't out-classed the rest of the league as much as we did this year," Larry said. Flint could see that he was nervous. "It's hard for anyone to tell how good you are when the other team's really not all that hot."

"Just think of them as the Islanders," Flint advised. "Pour on the coal each time you're out there. Believe me, the scouts will be impressed." Larry's darting, wheeling, high-powered game really was an attention-getter. Any major league hockey scout would see that, no matter who the other team was. Larry smiled doubtfully and moved on to greet the incoming guests.

Flint knew his own game wasn't a flashy one. His play was steady. Solid. But not flashy. He really couldn't see himself drawing the scout's attention in a positive way.

It's better to play your regular game, he decided, and if anything, just make sure you don't look bad.

Wednesday evening, Flint was the first player to walk into the Mantas' dressing room. He was putting on his uniform trunks when coach Carpenter put his head in the door.

"Have you heard Bronco Horvath is going to be here tonight?"

"Horvath?" Flint echoed.

"The scout for the Red Wings."

Flint nodded. "To see Larry."

"There's that," Carpenter agreed, "but he's here to see hockey players, period. He came in for a talk this afternoon, and he saw our scoreboard on the wall."

Bob Carpenter kept track of who was on the ice each time the Mantas scored. Those players each got a plus. But he also gave a minus to each player who was on the ice when the other team scored. Since he kept the scoreboard on the dressing room wall, the whole team knew who was playing offense and who was playing defense when it counted.

"He asked me about you, since you were seven pluses up on everyone else," Carpenter continued. "I told him you were maybe Number 45 on my list of fast skaters since I've been coaching here." He grinned suddenly. "But I also told him you get the job done. So get out there and get it done tonight." He went back to his office.

Flint drew a long, slow breath. Suddenly his feelings toward tonight's game had changed. He knew now why Larry felt nervous about coming under the watchful eye of the scout, Horvath. So much depended upon being called up to an NHL team. Flint didn't want to be sentenced to another year in junior league hockey. This was the first sign, though, that he might have a real chance to move up.

The Mantas had only two games left in their season. It might come down to what happened on the ice tonight. Horvath almost surely had other assignments on this scouting trip. It might even be a case of showing something tonight or waiting a long time for another chance.

The first ten minutes of the game against the Cardiff Bombers passed without much happening. Both teams blunted each other's rushes down the ice. The Mantas pressed a little more deeply than the Bombers but failed to score.

Then a Cardiff winger pulled down Bryan, as he was flashing past him, and the winger received a two-minute penalty. An expectant hum rose from the crowd. The referee prepared to slam the puck down into the Cardiff left face-off circle. With the one-man advantage, the Mantas placed themselves inside the Bombers' blue line. Flint planted himself a few feet from the left boards. He was prepared to keep the puck from crossing the blue line and putting his team offside.

The puck bounced from Larry's centering stab to Emile, who at once sent it across the ice to Flint. Flint wound up and fired a hard slap shot at the partially screened Cardiff goalie. Larry, who had skated to the crease in front of the net, deflected Flint's shot with his stick. The puck's change of direction caught the goaltender going the wrong way. The puck wound up in the back of the net, and the frustrated goalie fished it out with his stick.

Before the end of the period, Hank Wilson and Roy Eberhardt of the Mantas' second line each scored a goal. With a minute left, Tom Pollock misjudged a half-hit Cardiff shot and it trickled into his goal. The period ended with the score 3–1, Mantas.

Cardiff came out stronger in the second period. One of their defensemen stepped into Larry, who fell heavily. On his way down, though, he shoveled the puck to Bryan, who beat the surprised Cardiff goaltender with a low shot to his stick side. The Mantas' second line swung over the boards onto the ice again. Flint skated to the bench.

His thoughts drifted for a moment, even while he watched the play in front of him. He turned to see if he could locate the scout, who would be sitting behind the

Mantas' bench. His eyes focused upon a barrel-chested man with iron-gray hair, closely watching the game. That would be Bronco Horvath.

A groan from the crowd drew Flint's attention to the game again. Tom Pollock was rising from the ice, with the puck in the net behind him. Cardiff had scored. Tom was not having a very sharp night, Flint thought. Twice, Flint had seen Tom leave his feet too soon and flop around on the ice.

It happened again near the end of the period. Following a Cardiff rush, their left winger took a long shot. Flint put his shoulder into the chest of the opposing center and rode him away from a possible rebound. It didn't matter, though. The long shot landed two feet in front of Tom and bounced into the net on his glove side. The score was now 4–3, Mantas. A lot less comfortable than 4–1.

Coach Carpenter put Carl Dupont in goal at the start of the third period. Carl was a stand-up goalie who rarely went down on the ice. Flint concentrated on crashing his body into any Cardiff player who tried to get in the crease in front of Carl. He prevented Cardiff players from getting shots on the net.

The game came down to its final minutes, with the Mantas still leading, 4–3. Then Larry found himself with a shot at a wide-open net, after a scramble in front of the Cardiff goal. Instead of shooting, Larry passed backward to Flint, who had been trailing the play. Although surprised,

Flint fired almost from habit. It was a blistering shot that slammed the back of the net. The game ended two minutes later. Larry had let Flint score the final goal of the game.

"Thanks," Flint said to Larry in the dressing room afterward. Larry nodded. "Anything from Horvath?" Flint asked.

"I'm having coffee with him in an hour," Larry replied. "I'm more nervous now than I was before the game."

"Why worry?" Flint asked. "You're a player, and he had to see it. I don't even need to wish you good luck. You're on your way, man."

During his walk home to Mrs. Fox's, Flint tried to forget his disappointment at not having also been asked to have coffee with Bronco Horvath.

"Telephone, Flint!" Mrs. Fox called through Flint's bedroom door the next morning. Flint jumped into his robe and ran downstairs. The sun was barely up.

"This is Carpenter, Flint," the coach's harsh voice said in Flint's ear. "Horvath is having breakfast at the hotel coffee shop. He wants to talk to you right now. Get over there fast, because he's on his way out of town."

Flint ran back upstairs and dressed quickly. He also ran every step of the way downtown to the Hotel Raymond Coffee Shop. Inside, the burly-looking Bronco Horvath was seated at a corner table. "Sit down, Redmond," he said warmly, when

Flint came up to him. "Order up," he added when Flint sat down.

Flint looked at the ham and eggs and fried potatoes on Horvath's plate. "I'll have the same," Flint said to the waitress. "But only half of what he has."

Horvath looked up from beneath heavy eyebrows when the waitress left. "I noticed you played differently in front of your two goalies last night," he said.

Flint nodded. "They're different types. Tom's a flopper who almost always makes the first save. But he gives up a lot of rebounds. So I take the first man into the crease out of there completely, so he can't get a shot at a rebound."

"Carl," Flint continued, "is a stand-up type with a good glove who seldom gives up a rebound. With him, I concentrate on bothering all foreign bodies in the crease, so that no one gets a close-in shot at him."

Horvath raised his eyebrows. "Would you believe there have been guys who have come up to the bigs, played their seven or eight years, and retired without even practicing that little bit of defense work?" He went on before Flint could speak. "Carpenter tells me you're the hardest worker on the team."

"I'd like to think I am," Flint replied.

"So I'll lay it on the line for you," Horvath said. "I like some of the things you do. There are other things you may never be able to do for the big team. One is taking the point on a power play because you don't skate that well. There are some things that you'll need better coaching on, as Carpenter himself would tell you. But a worker can improve himself."

He waved his fork at Flint. "I can't make an outright recommendation in your case, as I can with Larry Russo. But I'm going to bring my boss back here for your final league game Friday night. That means you can do some selling on the ice while I'm doing it in the stands."

"What—what could it mean?" Flint asked hopefully.

"If you show him what you showed me last night, I'm sure he'll tell me to bring you up to the Wings for a tryout in the late summer. After that it gets harder. It depends on you. At first, I think you'd need to drop down to a team in the

American Hockey League, to get more
playing time and learn what you need to
know. That's for the first season."

"I'll learn," Flint promised. "I'll skate
all summer to be ready for camp."

"And there's always the chance some-
one will get hurt on the Wings. Then, if
you're doing well in the AHL you could be
pulled back up earlier. It just about all
depends on you." Horvath looked at his
watch. "Okay, got to run. See you Friday,
and I'll hope to see you again at camp."

He rose from the table and walked
quickly to the door.

Flint ate his breakfast while repeating
to himself everything Horvath had told
him.

He couldn't wait for Friday night to
come.

When it did come, Flint had butterflies in his stomach. He tried to tell himself it was just another game. But he knew that wasn't true. No game he'd ever played in had as much riding on it as this one did.

To make matters worse the team started poorly. They were playing the Dover Royals, who had speed. Tom Pollock again started off badly in goal. He gave up two quick scores on shots from beyond the blue line. *At least they weren't shots for which a defenseman could be blamed,* Flint thought. He then felt angry at himself for thinking that way. Tom was trying just as hard to impress Bronco Horvath and Bronco's boss as Flint was.

Tom settled down then, and he began

playing better. Bryan and Larry combined on an ice-length rush that got one of the goals back. Flint concentrated, during each of his turns on the ice, on playing good position. He skated a tight zone, not permitting an onrushing forward to skate around him or fake him to one side or the other.

The Mantas played a better game in the second period. Hank and Roy were flying up and down the ice, and soon the score was tied. Flint settled down to body-checking everything that moved in front of him. "Taking the sting out of them," coach Carpenter called it. And the Royals did slow down. They weren't rushing into the Mantas' end the way they had in the first period.

Slowly the Mantas' offense picked up. Larry led a series of attacks upon the Royals' goal. Frenchy and Bryan were perfect partners. Frenchy dug the puck out of the right corner and passed it to Bryan, who zipped it to Larry at the left goal mouth. Larry banged it home, and the Mantas took the lead, 3–2.

The third period was more of the same. Tom Pollock didn't permit the Royals to score again. And Flint, trailing a Mantas' rush, knocked down a pass from Emile, wheeled, and looked for his teammates. No one was as close to the goal as Flint was.

"Shoot! Shoot!" he could hear Larry calling. Flint fended off a Royals' defenseman with his left arm and shot with his right. The shot didn't have too much on it, but it squeezed between the goalie's left arm and the goal post. *Better to be lucky than good*, Flint thought.

Bronco Horvath called Flint over to the rinkside boards when the game ended. "This is my boss, Mr. Clark, the Red Wings' director of scouting," Horvath said.

"We'll look forward to seeing you at camp," Mr. Clark told Flint. "Try to put on fifteen pounds before we see you again. You're a bit light for the heavy-duty work I saw tonight."

"Fifteen pounds of muscle," Bronco added. "Not milk shakes. Get into a weight room." Mr. Clark nodded pleasantly and turned away. Bronco leaned over the boards and spoke to Flint in a low voice. "And don't forget the skating."

"I won't," Flint promised.

He watched while Bronco and Mr. Clark headed up the aisle in the direction of coach Carpenter's office.

Well, Flint Redmond, you wanted a shot at the bigs, and now you've got it.

He knew it was up to him now. And he wouldn't have it any other way.